THE EXTRAORDINARY FILES

he Headless Ghost

Paul Blum

RISING ★ STARS

It is th le.'

nasen

NASEN House, 4/5 Amber Business Village, Amber Close,
Amington, Tamworth, Staffordshire B77 4RP

Rising Stars UK Ltd.
22 Grafton Street, London W1S 4EX
www.risingstars-uk.com

Text © Rising Stars UK Ltd.
The right of Paul Blum to be identified as the author of this work has
been asserted by him in accordance with the Copyright, Design and
Patents Act 1988.

Published 2007
Reprinted 2008

Cover design: Button plc
Illustrator: Enzo Troiano
Text design and typesetting: pentacor**big**
Publisher: Gill Budgell
Project management and editorial: Lesley Densham
Editor: Maoliosa Kelly
Editorial consultant: Lorraine Petersen

British Library Cataloguing in Publication Data.
A CIP record for this book is available from the British Library.

ISBN: 978 1 84680 173 0

Printed by Craft Print International Limited, Singapore

CHAPTER ONE

The train went through the red light. The driver didn't even try to put his brakes on. The train was going so fast that it came off the rails.

When they found the driver, he was dead.
His head was cut off his body. There was a look
of terror in his eyes.

Night and day, the ghost walked up and down the
crash tunnel, screaming and moaning. The train
drivers all saw it. They had no doubt who the ghost
was. It was the ghost of their dead friend.

Soon the drivers would not drive trains down the Tolgate tunnel. They were too frightened.

Laura Turnbull and Robert Parker were detectives in the British Secret Service. They were put onto the case of the headless ghost.

On their first morning, they took a walk down the Tolgate Tunnel.

"Watch your head, Laura," Parker said.

"Stop fussing, Robert," she replied.

"So what are we doing down here?" he asked.

"We are looking for clues," Turnbull said.

"Ghosts don't leave clues," Parker replied.

Agent Parker shone his torch around the tunnel. "I hate rats," he said.

"And I hate mud all over my new shoes," Agent Turnbull replied.

"This place gives me the creeps. Let's go and see the Station Manager."

They found the station manager in his office.

"Can we see the accident reports?" Parker asked.

They read through the reports silently.

"Am I right in thinking that the Tolgate Tunnel is a new underground line?" Turnbull asked.

"You are, Miss," said the station manager. "It will go to the New Water Park, which is being built on wasteland, by the river. It is part of the London Millennium Project."

"What can you tell us about last week's train crash?" asked Parker.

"I have nothing to say. I don't know what is going on here. Take the reports away with you," said the station manager. "Then go and talk to the drivers."

CHAPTER TWO

Turnbull and Parker went to the drivers'
locker room. They found three drivers
playing cards. Turnbull stopped their game.

"Can we talk about the ghost?" she asked.

They looked frightened.

"Was the dead driver a good friend?"
she demanded.

"Look, lady. We have nothing to say,"
snapped one of the drivers, rising from
his seat. The rest put their cards down
and left the room.

Parker was puzzled. "They weren't very
helpful," he said.

Turnbull slammed her hand on the table
angrily.

"That station manager was trying to waste
our time," she said. "Let's go and check out
the New Water Park for ourselves."

The agents drove to the New Water Park. It was a strange place. In the middle was a big lake. Around the lake were three fountains that looked like snakes. The place was half-finished. There were bulldozers and cranes everywhere. Under the floodlights it was very silent and spooky.

Turnbull shivered. She checked the computer on her mobile phone.

"It says these are the biggest fountains in the world," she said. "They should make quite a splash when they come on."

"The whole park is big money," Parker said. "Look at all the new shops and offices they are building."

"Big money can mean big trouble. Maybe somebody doesn't want the train tunnel to come here," said Turnbull thoughtfully. "Maybe the headless ghost is part of a plan to stop them."

The agents jumped when they heard a sudden movement behind them.

"Who's there?" Turnbull shouted.

"Jenkins, the train driver," a strange voice whispered.

"What can we do for you?" Turnbull asked.

He handed her a log book.

"Check this out," he said. "You will find some clues about the headless ghost."

He ran off into the darkness before they could ask him any questions.

But someone else had been watching Jenkins.

Suddenly, Parker and Turnbull heard the noise of water. They rushed to the fountain but they got there too late. Train driver Jenkins could be of no more help to them. He was dead.

Turnbull told Parker to check the driver's pockets. Suddenly, the fountain came on again. Turnbull grabbed Parker and pulled him back.

"It was a trap," he gasped.

"And I saved your suit, Parker," she said.

"More than my suit, Agent Turnbull. With 100 gallons of water on my head, I would have needed the undertaker, not the dry cleaners," he replied.

Turnbull pulled out her mobile.

"I'm calling in forensic. They can check this place out for clues. We can do no more here for the moment," she said.

CHAPTER THREE

The next morning, Turnbull dragged Parker up onto the roof of a tall building. The building looked down onto the River Thames.

"Why are we up here, Laura? You know I'm scared of heights," said Parker.

"Agent Parker, seeing is believing," said Turnbull.

"I'm keeping my eyes closed."

"Open them,"

"I'm too dizzy."

"Open them or I will let go of your hand."

"OK, have mercy."

"So what do you see?"

"A large flat roof with a 300 foot drop onto water."

"But do you see the big boat, just there?"

"Yeah, very nice."

"The person who owns it is called Ray Rogers. He wants to run passenger boats up and down the river from Tolgate to the New Water Park," said Turnbull.

Parker got excited at the name Ray Rogers.

"Rogers is the man who owns the company that is laying the rails on the new Tolgate Tunnel. I checked him out in the log book which Jenkins gave us," he said.

"Sailing boats and building railways to the same place. This man has got his finger in every pie. Something is not right here," Turnbull replied. "We need to see Mr Rogers."

They took a rowing boat out to Ray Rogers' big boat on the river. A bouncer showed them into a very big office.

Ray Rogers was working at his desk. His dogs growled when the agents came in. Parker was so frightened that he could not move. Turnbull just kept walking.

"This is all very impressive," she said, looking around.

"I would have tidied up if I had known you were coming," he replied, smiling at her. "To what do I owe this pleasure, young lady?"

"I want to ask you about your business,"
Turnbull replied.

"And who exactly are you?" said Rogers.

"I am Agent Turnbull and this is my partner,
Agent Parker," said Turnbull.

"Do you expect me to talk to two coppers?" sneered Rogers.

"We are not the police. We work for the government," said Turnbull.

"And I work for myself," Rogers replied sharply.

"We are working on a murder case," said Turnbull and she stared at Rogers.

"That must be nice for you," said Rogers and his eyes narrowed.

"We would like to ask you about your river boat plan," said Turnbull.

"It was turned down," he said angrily.

Turnbull gave him a very hard stare.

"So now you are trying to stop the tunnel project. You asked your men to break the rails that they were laying. A driver has died and a so-called ghost is scaring all the workers. Where will it end?" she shouted at him.

"What has all this got to do with me?" Rogers sneered.

"Just answer the questions," Turnbull said sharply.

"I have had enough of this. Come back when you have some proof. I want you off my boat now!" Rogers shouted at her. His tanned face was red with anger.

The dogs growled again. Parker went white with
fear but Turnbull ignored them.

"We will be back, Mr Rogers," Turnbull said as she
turned and walked away.

"Not unless you want to swim out here," he shouted
after her.

27

CHAPTER FOUR

It was difficult for the two agents now. They had no proof and they had made Rogers very angry.

Turnbull took Parker down into the Tolgate Tunnel again to look for clues. Parker was not happy.

"It's cold down here, Laura. I should have worn my gloves," he said. Suddenly they heard the sound of mad laughter. A ghostly figure came towards them.

Parker screamed.

"It's the headless ghost! I'm getting out of here!"

He ran off into the darkness, dropping his torch.
The ghost followed him.

Turnbull was left on her own. Suddenly she heard the sound of rails humming.

"It's a train!" she screamed. "But they said they had shut down the line!"

She looked round. She had only seconds to live or die. She lay down on the line. The train passed just over her head.

A minute later she got up. She was alive! But where was Parker? She went to look for him in the tunnel.

It was then she came upon the headless ghost.
He was sitting by one of the fountains.

Turnbull jumped him from behind.

"You're nicked!" she shouted in his ear.

"Get off me," begged the ghost. "You're pulling my head off."

"So where is my partner?" she demanded.

"The one who is scared of ghosts?" he sneered.

"Don't mess about. Just answer the questions," she said.

He told her that Parker was held prisoner and said he would take her to him.

CHAPTER FIVE

They went back up the Tolgate Tunnel again.

The ghost took her to the underground train park. There was one carriage with lights on. Turnbull tied up the headless ghost and then crept towards the door of the carriage. When she went in she saw Parker on his own. But before they had a chance to get away, Rogers and his men blocked the door.

"So we meet again," Rogers sneered.

"I must warn you. Holding a government agent as a prisoner is a very serious crime. You do not have to say anything but anything you do say . . ." Turnbull started to read Rogers his rights.

Rogers and his men just fell about laughing. Rogers came towards Turnbull. When he tried to grab her, Turnbull got him in an armlock. She was about to swing him around when everybody froze.

The carriage had started to shake. There was a sound of moaning and screaming. Everyone, even Rogers, looked worried.

"What's going on?" he shouted.

"It must be the ghost," Parker said.

"Cut it out, mate. I know all the spooks in this tunnel," said Rogers. He put his hand over his mouth. He knew he had given himself away.

Rogers and his men tried to run away but they were stopped by the police.

The train drivers had been rocking the carriage and making ghostly noises. As Rogers and his men were led away, the train drivers cheered.

CHAPTER SIX

About one hour later, Turnbull and Parker left Tolgate
tube station.

"Do you want a lift?" Parker asked.

"Do I have a choice?" she said.

"You could buy a ticket. Take the tube," he joked.

She didn't see the funny side of it. She was still thinking of the train going over her.

"We did very well," he said, trying to cheer her up.

"I wanted to get him for what he did."

"Come on, Agent Turnbull — temper, temper. Remember, you are a highly-trained professional."

It was Friday night. It was time to relax for the weekend. They could not agree about where to go and what to do. Parker wanted to have a drink and a sandwich.

Turnbull looked at him as if he were mad. "I want my hair done. I want to go shopping and spend lots of money," she told him.

Parker asked her if she wanted to go out on Saturday evening for some fun.

"Fun — you don't know what the word means!" she said.

Parker looked sad as he watched her turn off her mobile until Monday morning. They went their separate ways for the weekend.

GLOSSARY OF TERMS

bouncer a person whose job is to throw troublesome people out

coppers policemen

detective person who investigates crimes

forensic department which collects scientific evidence for legal use

locker room room with cupboards for clothes

nicked caught

record book book recording details of journeys and incidents

Secret Service Government Intelligence Department

spooks ghosts

to have a finger in every pie to be involved in lots of different things

to read someone his rights to arrest someone

undertaker person whose job is to arrange funerals

QUIZ

1 Where did the accident happen?

2 Who gave Agent Turnbull the log book?

3 What happened to train driver Jenkins?

4 Who wants to run passenger boats from Tolgate to the Water Park?

5 Who is building the railway from Tolgate to the Water Park?

6 Is the headless ghost real? How do you know?

7 Who is afraid of ghosts?

8 What happens to Agent Turnbull in the tunnel?

9 What happens to Ray Rogers in the end?

10 What does Parker want to eat at the end of the story?

ABOUT THE AUTHOR

Paul Blum has taught for over twenty years in London inner-city schools.

I wrote The Extraordinary Files for my pupils so they've been tested by some fierce critics (you!). That's why I know you'll enjoy reading them.

I've made the stories edgy in terms of character and content and I've written them using the kind of fast-paced dialogue you'll recognise from television soaps. I hope you'll find The Extraordinary Files an interesting and easy-to-read collection of stories.

ANSWERS TO QUIZ

1 In the Tolgate Tunnel

2 Train driver Jenkins

3 He was drowned in the snake fountains

4 Ray Rogers

5 Ray Rogers

6 No. He is a real man, employed by Ray Rogers to frighten the drivers.

7 The train drivers. Agent Parker.

8 She has to lie down between the tracks while a train goes over her.

9 He is arrested.

10 He wants to eat a sandwich.